★ THE ADVENTURES OF ★
TINTIN

THE ADVENTURES OF TINTIN: THE MYSTERY OF THE MISSING WALLETS
A BANTAM BOOK 978 0 857 51073 0

First published in the United States in 2011 by Little Brown

First published in Great Britain by Bantam,
an imprint of Random House Children's Books
A Random House Group Company

Bantam edition published 2011

1 3 5 7 9 10 8 6 4 2

Bantam Books are published by Random House Children's Books,
61–63 Uxbridge Road, London W5 5SA

www.**kids**at**randomhouse**.co.uk
www.**totallyrandombooks**.co.uk
www.**randomhouse**.co.uk

Addresses for companies within The Random House Group Limited can be found at: www.randomhouse.co.uk/offices.htm

THE RANDOM HOUSE GROUP Limited Reg. No. 954009

A CIP catalogue record for this book is available from the British Library.

Printed in Great Britain by Print 4 Limited.

★ THE ADVENTURES OF ★
TINTIN

THE MYSTERY OF THE MISSING WALLETS

Adapted by Kirsten Mayer

Screenplay by Steven Moffat

and Edgar Wright & Joe Cornish

Based on The Adventures of Tintin series by Hergé

BANTAM BOOKS

WALLET

CANE

BOWLER HAT

Tintin and his dog, Snowy,
like to find clues and solve crimes.
They work with the police all the time.

Tintin works with a pair of policemen
named Thomson and Thompson.
They look alike, but they are not twins.
They are not even brothers.

Thomson and Thompson visit Tintin
and tell him about a criminal on the loose.
"A pickpocket," explains Thompson.
"He has no idea what is coming!"

"What do you mean?" asks Tintin.

Thomson holds open his coat.

"Go on. Take my wallet," he tells the boy.

Tintin takes the wallet

out of Thomson's pocket.

The wallet snaps right back!

The wallet is attached to the coat with a cord.

"Very resourceful," says Tintin.

"Simply childish," says Thomson.

"Childishly simple," corrects Thompson.

The policemen tip their bowler hats to Tintin and take off down the street into the fog.

"I expect he is miles away by now," says Thomson.

"The pickpocket?" his partner asks. Thomson nods.

An older gentleman walks towards
Thomson and Thompson.
He is the pickpocket!
As he brushes past them,
he slides his hand into Thomson's pocket.

He grabs the wallet and walks away,
but the pickpocket is yanked back
by the elastic!
"I have got you now!" yells Thomson.

The pickpocket lets go.
The wallet snaps back
into Thomson's face.

Thompson grabs the criminal's jacket.

He calls out, "Stop in the name of the law!"

But the thief shrugs out of the jacket

and flips it over Thompson's head.

Thompson stumbles into a lamp post,

tripping up Thomson, too!

Tintin and Snowy hear the shouting.

Snowy growls.

"What's going on?" asks Tintin.

"Come on, Snowy."

They rush down the street
and bump into an older man
hurrying the other way!
"I beg your pardon, sir,"
says the stranger.

Tintin and Snowy find
the policemen on the ground.
"The pickpocket is getting away!"
yells Thomson.
Tintin realizes that he bumped
into the criminal!
He checks his pocket. Snowy barks.

"My wallet is gone!" cries Tintin.

"I have to get it back!"

"You will," says Thompson.

"Leave it to the professionals."

The next day, Thomson and Thompson pay a visit to a man at his home. "Mr Silk?" asks Thompson.

"We pulled a jacket off a thief," explains Thomson, "and your wallet was inside." Silk is the thief, but they do not recognize him!

They return the wallet.

"That is my wallet," admits Silk.

"It must have been stolen from you," says Thompson.

"May we come in?" asks Thomson.

"Oh, no need to come in!" says Silk.

"We insist!" says Thomson.

The policemen follow Silk.
Inside Silk's apartment,
the shelves are filled with wallets!
"Good grief! What is all this?"
asks Thompson.

"It is my collection," says Silk.
"It started with coin purses.
I cannot help it."

"You want to be careful," says Thompson.
"There is a pickpocket loose!
A master criminal! A wallet-lifting thief!"
"I am not a bad man!" protests Silk.

Thompson finds a wallet on the shelf.
"Look at this! It says *Thompson* on it!"
Thomson holds up another wallet.
"No, it is *Thomson* without a *p*,
as in the word *psychic*."

"You have it wrong," says Thompson.

"There is a *p* in *psychic*."

"I am not your sidekick," argues Thomson, not hearing his friend clearly. "You are mine."

"I met you first," says Thompson.

"No, you did not," says Thomson.

"Yes, I did," says Thompson.

"Did not!" "Did!" "Did not!"

The thief breaks down.

"I cannot stand it any more!" he tells them.

"I will come quietly."

Silk fills their arms with wallets.

"Take them all!" he shouts.

"Good heavens," says Thomson.

"This wallet looks familiar. Is it?"

"It is!" agrees Thompson. "Tintin!"

Thomson and Thompson solve the mystery,
and they return Tintin's wallet right away.
Thompson smiles at their friend and says,
"It is right here in the paper.
That pocket picker has picked his last pocket!"